The Courageous Cats' Club

Steve Wood

Illustrations by Woody Fox

D1390492

LION
Children's Books

Sticks and Stones

Contents

1

⁂

Leaving Home

Douglas had it all worked out. He would sit in his new garden with his new friends and tell them stories about the place where he was born.

Tales of the enchanted island he came from. He would tell them about the little people who wear red caps and green jackets and who get up to all kinds of mischief. He would tell them about the ruined castle that is haunted by a big black dog. And, of course, he would tell them about kippers, the special kind of fish he always liked to eat for his supper.

As the ship pulled away from the harbour, Douglas gazed out of his cat basket and took a last look at the island. The sun was shining on the long row of brightly coloured hotels along the sea front. He watched as the pinks and yellows and reds and blues slowly melted into one so that the buildings now looked like a huge stick of seaside rock. Douglas was going to miss the island so much. He had always lived in a small town by the sea, but now he was going to live in a huge city. His owner, Sarah, had got a new job, which meant that she had to move house.

When Douglas first heard the news he tried to be excited about it, but he couldn't. Then he tried to be happy because he loved Sarah and she was taking him with her, but he couldn't do that either. All Douglas felt was sadness because he knew that once he left the island he would never see his mum again. Douglas thought about the last time he had seen her. They had sat together under the garden bench, with the rain hammering against the seat above their heads. The thunder was rumbling and the wind was howling, but they were dry and safe.

'You're very lucky,' his mum said. 'Not many cats from the Isle of Man have the chance to go and live in London.'

Douglas snuggled up to her. His mum's fur

always seemed to be warm.

'I don't feel lucky, I feel sad.'

'Sadness is like the rain,' she said. 'It doesn't last for ever. Sometimes when it's raining you think it's never going to stop, but it always does and at last the sun comes out.'

Douglas remembered how he had run out from under the bench and darted frantically around the garden. His mum called for him to come back for shelter, but he just ran round and round in the pouring rain, shouting at the top of his voice:

'Rain, rain, wash away my sorrow,
Please let the sun come out tomorrow!'
His heart was thumping and he was becoming
more and more breathless, but he ran faster and
faster and shouted louder and louder:
'Rain, rain, wash away my sorrow,
Please let the sun come out tomorrow!'
Then he scurried back under the bench. He
was soaking wet and gasping for breath, but
somehow his mad dash had made him feel better.
The rain did stop in the end just as his mum had
said it would, and it had been sunny ever since.

Now the sun was beating down on the deck of
the ship and the island was a distant blur on the
horizon. Douglas suddenly felt very lonely. He
didn't know any cats in London and the more he
thought about living there, the more frightened
he became. Once again he tried to think nice
thoughts. He imagined that he was sitting in his
new garden with his new friends, telling them all
about the place where he was born.

'I come from the Isle of Man.'

'The Isle of *what?*'

'The Isle of Man. It's in the middle of the Irish

Sea, halfway between England and Ireland. I'm a Manx cat.'

'A *what*?'

'A Manx cat. Anything from the Isle of Man is called Manx.'

As the sea gently rocked the ship, Douglas nodded off and dreamed of all the wonderful new friends he was going to meet in London. He dreamed of them playing together and chatting together and getting along just fine. It was a nice dream, but would it come true?

2

···

The Courageous Cats' Club

It was another very hot day in London. In the shade of the apple tree at the bottom of Bertie's garden, the Courageous Cats' Club was about to meet for the first time.

'The early bird catches the worm,' said Clive. He had made himself the leader of the club because it had been his idea and because he was the oldest.

He had big eyes, big legs and a big tail that always stuck up in the air and made him seem even bigger. He was black all over apart from a blaze of white fur down the middle of his face and some long, white whiskers. Clive wasn't like most cats. He didn't enjoy spending his time washing and grooming himself, which was obvious from his somewhat scruffy appearance. He didn't particularly like lying around in the garden or snoozing in the sun and he didn't think it was much fun to chase birds – probably because he couldn't catch them any more. He was an old cat and the days when he would have caught any bird that dared to visit his garden were long gone.

Although Clive was a bit slower than he used to be, he still liked to keep busy. Setting up the Courageous Cats' Club was his latest plan to keep himself and his friends occupied throughout the summer months.

Last summer he had come up with the Charcoal Club to steal fish from Mr Wright's barbecue. It was a disaster, and the only free food they got was when Mr Wright threw an onion at Clive and knocked him off the wall. Before that it was the Fencing Club, when Clive, Bertie and Camilla had tried to see how many garden fences they could squeeze under without getting stuck. Unfortunately, Bertie became wedged under Mrs Russell's fence and had to be freed by a neighbour. And of course there was the Hose Pipe Club – but the less said about that, the better.

'The early bird catches the worm,' said Clive again. 'And the early cat catches the bird,' he added dramatically.

He paced round and round the apple tree muttering to himself. The Courageous Cats' Club had not got off to the best of starts because nobody else had turned up for the meeting. Nobody, that is, until Tiger scampered across the lawn.

'Hi Clive!'

Clive was going to tell him off for being late, but Tiger was only a kitten and he didn't want to upset him.

'Hello Tiger.'

'Where are all the others?'

'They will be here soon.'

Tiger was a tiny ginger cat with lovely, soft fur. He had pale, narrow stripes running down from his spine round to his tummy.

'I've never been in a club before,' said Tiger, and his right ear began to twitch, as it always did when he became excited.

Tiger had heard stories about the other clubs, but they had all come and gone before he was born. Now, at last, it was time for him to attend his first ever club meeting.

'What's the club called?' asked Tiger. 'I've forgotten.'

'The Courageous Cats' Club,' said Clive proudly.

'What's a Courageous Cat?'

Clive lazily swiped a paw in the air to shoo away a butterfly that was dancing around his head.

'A Courageous Cat,' he said, 'is a cat with courage. A cat that shows bravery in any and every situation.'

'Are you talking about me again?' said Bertie as he strolled into the shade of the apple tree. 'Sorry I'm late – had a spot of bother finding the place,' he added with a yawn.

'But this is your garden!' said Tiger.

Bertie looked around. 'So it is,' he said. 'So it is.'

Tiger laughed. He never knew if Bertie was being serious or not.

Bertie was a fat white cat with large patches of red, cream and black fur. Around his eyes perfect circles of black fur gave the impression that he wore glasses.

'Is it just the three of us?' asked Bertie, looking around and peering through his spectacles.

'So far,' said Clive. 'Camilla is the last to get here as usual.'

'I was here before any of you,' said a voice.

Clive, Bertie and Tiger looked up into the apple tree and there, draped over a branch, was Camilla, sunbathing.

'How long have you been there?' asked Clive, suddenly caught off his guard.

'Long enough to have heard you talking to yourself,' said Camilla.

'I was not talking to myself,' snapped Clive.

'That's what it sounded like to me.'

'Can we start now?' asked Tiger, his right ear twitching rapidly.

'Why don't you all come up here?' said Camilla. 'We can hold the meeting in the apple tree. It's lovely and warm in the sun.'

'Don't be ridiculous,' said Clive.

Clive and Camilla were heading for a fight. Tiger hated to watch them fighting and did his best to keep the peace.

'Why don't we have the first meeting down here and the next one up there?' he suggested hopefully.

'I might decide not to hold another meeting,' said Clive.

'It's not up to you,' said Camilla. 'Isn't that right, Bertie?'

'I'm not discussing the next meeting before we've started this one,' said Bertie. 'So come on, Camilla, be a sport and get on down here.'

Camilla slowly got to her feet. Knowing that all the others were watching her, she enjoyed a long, slow stretch of her sleek, slender body. Her face and legs were the colour of clotted cream and her nose, ears and tail were a warm, apricot colour. Camilla always took great pride in her appearance and looked as beautiful as ever.

'As leader of the Courageous Cats' Club,' said Clive, 'it is my duty to open the first meeting by making a speech.'

This was something he always did and something which Bertie and Camilla dreaded because Clive usually rambled on for ages about club rules.

Camilla dropped silently out of the tree, closely followed by an apple which she had accidentally dislodged. She landed on the lawn, the apple landed on Bertie's head and the meeting was closed because Bertie had to go home with a headache.

3

Into the Jungle

Douglas could hardly believe his eyes. He had
never seen such a big garden or one that was
so overgrown. It was a mass of greenery and it
looked as if all the trees and bushes and plants
were desperately clambering over each other
in a frantic race to get out. On one side of the
garden some ivy was climbing over a wall. On
the other side a rambling bush had smashed
through a rickety old garden fence and was
now working its way up a tree in the next-door
garden. Or was it in the next-door garden?
Douglas couldn't make out where his garden
ended and others began.

At the bottom of the garden some orange
flowers were scrambling over a high hedge,
while others seemed to be taking a shortcut

under it. What had once been the lawn was now a dense mass of long grass and even longer dandelions and thistles.

This was not how Douglas had imagined London to be. He had thought it would be full of dull, grey buildings and had worried that his new house might not have a garden. He could never have dreamed of one like this.

Douglas trotted down the three steps that led from the patio into the long grass and was immediately hit by the heat from the scorching sun. It was far too hot to be out in the open, so he decided to explore the hedges where it might be a little cooler.

Douglas crawled under a bush into the shade and the temperature was much more pleasant. He slowly picked his way through the under-growth, being careful not to scratch himself on the huge thorns of the wild roses all around him. The further he went, the darker it became and the cooler the earth felt under his paws. The ground was hard and dry, old twigs and leaves cracked under foot and every sound seemed to echo. A cloud of midges was dancing wildly above his head, so he ran further into the undergrowth to shake them off.

Now it was very dark and very quiet. Douglas suddenly felt quite cold and a shiver ran down his spine. It was then that he had the feeling that he was being watched. Douglas crouched down low, his head and body almost level with the ground. He pricked up his ears and without making a sound he carefully looked all around. Then he heard a rustle up ahead of him and saw a huge leaf move ever so slightly. Someone, or something, was watching him from behind a gigantic rhubarb plant. Douglas silently crawled on his stomach towards it. As he neared the big leafy plant, he stopped and got ready to pounce on his hidden victim. His bottom swung from side to side as he prepared to spring into the air, but just then a rhubarb leaf moved to one side to reveal a smiling ginger face.

'Hi,' said the ginger face.

Douglas was relieved that the stranger seemed small and friendly.

'I'm Tiger.'

As usual Douglas didn't know what to say

when he met someone he didn't know.

Tiger continued, 'Tigers can be found in the
jungle. That's what I call this place because it's
so overgrown.'

Douglas still couldn't think of anything to say,
but Tiger didn't have any such problem.

'I haven't seen you around here before.
What's your name? Where are you going?'

Douglas took a deep breath and gabbled
out the answers. 'I'm Douglas. I'm not going

anywhere, I'm exploring. I've just moved in.'

'To the jungle? You're the new owner?'

Douglas nodded nervously. He wasn't sure if Tiger approved of this or not.

'Then you've got a *lot* of exploring to do. I'll show you round if you like.'

Douglas could think of nothing he'd like less. Tiger seemed nice enough, but there would be so much talking to do and Douglas was worried that he wouldn't know what to say.

'Can I be your jungle guide, Douglas?'

Douglas looked at the little ginger face and noticed that its right ear was twitching.

'Can I?'

It was difficult to refuse. Douglas smiled and nodded.

'Great. Come on, follow me and watch out for these nettles.'

Tiger showed Douglas how to get into the garden shed through a broken window and the best place to go to play Bash the Bumble Bee, a game which he had invented. They saw a hedgehog under an old log, then they spotted a squirrel, but before they could decide whether they should chase it, it had gone.

They sat for a while in a rusty, old wheelbarrow and Tiger told Douglas about Fang, the big dog at Number 12.

He told him of the time that Fang chased him and cornered him near Mr Reynolds' garage.

'I thought he was going to eat me for his supper,' said Tiger, shaking at the thought of it. 'But he just barked at me and wandered off.'

'Perhaps he's a vegetarian,' said Douglas and they both laughed.

'Talking of food,' said Tiger, 'I'll have to go home for my lunch now, and then I'm going to have a nap.'

'Is it lunch time already?' asked Douglas. He hadn't realized that they had been exploring and talking all morning. 'Maybe we can do some more exploring tomorrow.'

'I can't tomorrow,' said Tiger. 'I'm going to a meeting.'

'A meeting?'

'Yes, I'm in a club,' said Tiger, trying to sound important. 'I'm a member of the… oh no, I've forgotten what it's called. Anyway, it's a club for brave cats. Would you like to come along? You can meet my friends, Clive, Camilla and Bertie.'

'I'm not sure,' said Douglas. The thought of meeting lots of new cats was making him nervous.

'We always meet in Bertie's garden at the end of the road. Under the apple tree. So you'll come then?'

Douglas couldn't think of an excuse.

'Great. See you at 10 o'clock tomorrow.' And with that Tiger set off for home.

Douglas watched the little ball of ginger fur bobbing up and down in the long grass until it vanished under the hedge at the bottom of the garden. Douglas had made his first new friend. If all the others are as nice as him, he thought, it's not going to be so bad after all.

4

Welcome to the Club

'I think our club should have a secret password,' suggested Tiger.

'We've already got one,' said Camilla.

'What is it?'

'I'm not telling you, it's a secret.'

Camilla burst out laughing at her own little joke and Bertie joined in with a loud cackle.

'I want to know the secret password,' said Tiger.

'Take no notice of her,' said Clive. 'She's just teasing you.'

The second meeting of the Courageous Cats' Club was under way. Douglas was listening from behind a wall near the apple tree. He had been there for ages, but had been too nervous to introduce himself. He knew that the longer he waited and thought about it the harder it would be. He knew that all he had to do was stroll up and say hello and in no time he'd have more new friends. But somehow it was never that easy.

Camilla let out another shriek of laughter, which was followed by a cackle from Bertie as usual. They were all having such a good time and Douglas wanted to be part of it. He hated being shy. He hated not knowing what to say to animals he'd never met before. He was fine once he got to know everybody, but until then he just couldn't cope. He either said too much and they thought he was a show-off, or he said too little and they thought he wasn't interested.

Sometimes he didn't say anything at all and they didn't know what to make of him.

'Just be yourself,' his mum used to say. 'When you meet somebody new, just be yourself.'

'Just be yourself,' Douglas said to himself.

He took a deep breath and climbed up onto the top of the wall and sat down with a big smile. The others didn't notice him – they were talking about famous courageous cats they had seen on TV. As the conversation continued Douglas became more and more worried. If they saw him now it would look as though he had been spying on them. He took a few more deep breaths and finally spoke.

'Hello.'

Nobody heard him. Or were they ignoring him? No, they just hadn't heard him.

Perhaps he had spoken too quietly. That often happened. Douglas was just about to give up and go home when Tiger spotted him.

'There you are!' he shouted. 'About time too!'

Clive, Camilla and Bertie stopped talking and turned to look at the stranger sitting on the wall.

Just be yourself, thought Douglas.

'Hello,' he repeated, as confidently as he could.

The cats stared at him in silence.

'I'm Douglas.'

Camilla giggled. 'Douglas? What kind of a name is that?'

'Douglas… is where I come from. I was named after the town where I was born.'

'I was born in Hackney,' said Clive. 'But

30

I don't expect you to call me that.'

Camilla laughed and Bertie cackled so loudly that he gave himself the hiccups. Douglas summoned all the courage he could find.

'Douglas is on the Isle of Man,' he said. 'I'll tell you about it if you like. I know a great story about…'

'We were all born in London,' snapped Clive. 'The most exciting city in the world. We don't give a fish's head about some silly little island.'

'I agree,' said Camilla.

Bertie tried to agree, but all that came out of his mouth was another hiccup.

Douglas decided to give it one last go. 'I know a great story about a castle that's haunted by a big black dog.'

Douglas jumped down from the wall and strolled onto the lawn trying to look confident. Suddenly Camilla let out an ear-piercing shriek which nearly made Tiger jump out of his skin with fright.

'Look!' she screamed in horror as she pointed a paw at Douglas. 'Look at him! Look at him!'

The cats stared at Douglas in disbelief. Clive,

for once, was speechless and Bertie was so shocked his hiccups stopped.

'Either I need new glasses or that cat has got no tail!' he gasped.

Douglas didn't know what to do. He didn't know whether to try to hide his bottom or carry on as if nothing had happened. The most appealing idea was to run home as quickly as possible and never come out of the house again.

Things were not going as he had planned. He wanted to tell stories to his new friends, but all they were bothered about was the fact that he didn't have a tail.

Tiger desperately tried to think of something to say. When they'd first met, he'd noticed that Douglas had no tail, but he didn't think anything of it. It didn't seem to bother Douglas and so it didn't bother him either. He didn't know why the others were making such a fuss. What difference did it make?

'What happened to your tail? Did you have an accident?' asked Tiger.

Douglas shook his head. 'No, I'm a Manx cat.'

'A what cat?'

'Manx. Anything that comes from the Isle of Man is called Manx. I'm a Manx cat and Manx cats don't have tails.'

'I've heard of such creatures,' said Bertie. 'But I never believed they actually existed.'

'I wish they didn't,' said Camilla. 'It's disgusting.'

'It's not disgusting!' shouted Douglas. 'I was born without a tail, that's all.'

'And you think that makes you special, do you?' said Clive, with a sneer.

'No. I'm just the same as all of you,' said Douglas.

'You are certainly not the same as me,' said Camilla and she flicked her whip-like tail from side to side. 'I have a beautiful long tail, not a stump. Now go away – I feel quite sick just looking at you.'

'Go on,' shouted Clive. 'Clear off!'

Douglas turned around and walked back towards the wall. He was heartbroken.

Clive shouted after him, 'Hey, Stumpy!'

Douglas stopped. 'Yes?' he asked quietly.

Clive laughed. 'Just as I thought,' he said to the others. 'That's his real name – Stumpy!'

Douglas scrambled up the wall, dropped to the ground in the next-door garden and started to run for home. He scurried through the neighbouring gardens, Clive and Camilla shouting 'Stumpy! Stumpy!' as he went. He climbed his garden fence and jumped down into the bushes. Still he ran, the tears welling up in his eyes. He darted through the undergrowth, out into the long grass and up the patio steps. By the time he reached the door to his house he was already in tears. He bashed through the cat flap, jumped into his basket, put his head under his blanket and cried all day.

5

:::

A Surprise Invitation

Douglas hardly went out of the house for a
whole week. When he did, he just sat on the
patio and stared at the overgrown garden,
longing for the sea view from his house on the
Isle of Man. He thought about trying to get
back there, but it was too far and he didn't know
the way. He'd once heard a story about a cat
who travelled hundreds of miles to get back to
his old house. He crossed motorways and rivers,
climbed hills and mountains, and finally arrived
home after three months. Douglas knew that he
could never do that – he didn't know whether to
turn left or right at the end of the road.

One morning as Douglas was sitting on the
patio, he spotted something out of the corner
of his eye. He wandered over to a stack of dirty

plant pots and lying beside them was the head of an old garden gnome. Just the head, nothing else. It had dark blue eyes, a chipped nose and a dirty beard with the end broken off.

'You look as sad as I feel,' said Douglas. 'You've got no friends either, have you? You've got nobody to play with. You've got nobody to talk to. In fact, you've got nobody at all.'

Douglas smiled. He had made a joke.

'No body, get it?'

The gnome's head stared back at him and suddenly Douglas felt sadder than ever. He hadn't even got a friend to share his joke.

'Hi Douglas.'

Sitting on top of the rickety fence was Tiger.

'Is it all right if I come into the jungle? I mean your garden.'

Douglas nodded. Tiger jumped down from the fence and climbed the steps to the patio and sat down.

'I'm sorry about what happened at the meeting.'

'You don't have anything to be sorry about,' said Douglas.

'I'm sorry my friends made fun of you. I don't know why they did that. To be honest, I think they were a bit scared.'

Douglas was confused. 'Why would they be scared of me?'

'Because... because you don't look the same as us.'

Douglas didn't say anything and the two of them sat in silence for a while.

Tiger could see that Douglas was very sad and he tried to cheer him up.

'Shall we do some more exploring?'

Douglas shook his head. 'No thanks, I'd rather be on my own. I quite like it. You might as well go back to your friends.'

'I haven't got any friends,' said Tiger.

'That lot in the club. Go and play with them.'

'I'm not in the club any more. I left. After you'd gone I said that if they wouldn't let you be in the club then I didn't want to be in it.'

Douglas turned to Tiger. 'You left because of me? You hardly even know me.'

'I know that you're a nice cat, a friendly cat. They didn't even wait to find that out. They decided they didn't like you just because you haven't got a tail, because you look a bit different.'

'There's nothing wrong with being different. We don't all have to be the same,' said Douglas. 'Besides, if they lived on the Isle of Man, *they* would be the ones that were different.'

Tiger laughed. 'I never thought of it like that.'

'What did they say when you said you were leaving the club?' asked Douglas.

'They didn't think I would do it, but I did. I didn't see any of them for days. I was all alone and I hated it.'

'I hate being alone too,' said Douglas quietly.

'This morning Clive came round to my house,' Tiger continued. 'He said that he and the others would like me to join the club again. I said I would, but only if they let you join too. Clive said that would be OK.'

'I don't want to join the club.'

'You want to have some friends, don't you?'

'I don't want friends like them,' said Douglas.

'They're all right when you get to know them. Clive's a big softy at heart, and Camilla and

Bertie are just a pair of clowns. You'll like them
when you get to know them.'

'I don't want to get to know them.'

'I understand,' said Tiger. '*We* can still be
friends though, can't we?'

Douglas nodded and Tiger leaped to his feet.

'Do you fancy a game of Bash the Bumble
Bee?'

'I can't remember how to play it.'

'I'll show you.'

'It's very hot to be chasing around,' protested
Douglas, but he was wasting his breath. Tiger
had already headed off towards a big bush full
of yellow flowers.

'Come on!'

The bush was covered in bees busying themselves and minding their own business. Suddenly Tiger leaped through the air to try to catch one of them, but they all saw him coming and simply flew out of the way. Tiger had another go, but again the bees calmly moved to another part of the bush and carried on doing whatever it is that bees do. Douglas couldn't catch one either.

Swiping one of them with a paw looked like the easiest thing in the world, but try as they might Tiger and Douglas couldn't get anywhere near the bees. The two cats tried sneaking up on them and then pouncing, they tried standing on their hind paws and clapping their front ones together, they tried everything they could think of, but after nearly an hour not one bee had been bashed.

The two cats lay down under a tree, exhausted.

'I think I might have to invent a new game,' said Tiger.

Douglas laughed. He felt as if he'd known

Tiger for years and yet he hardly knew him at all. He had been so easy to make friends with. He was chatty, pleasant and fun. He was... well, he was just Tiger. From the moment they had met Tiger had simply been himself. Douglas could hear his mother's voice in his head, saying, 'Just be yourself.'

'I'm going to the club meeting tomorrow,' said Tiger. 'I'd really like it if you came with me. Will you come?'

Douglas nodded. Tiger smiled. The bees buzzed.

6

Clive Sets a Test

'I understand that you two would like to join the Courageous Cats' Club,' said Clive.

Tiger and Douglas nodded. They were sitting next to each other beneath Bertie's apple tree. Opposite them was Clive with Bertie and Camilla on either side. Clive was very serious.

'To join the club you have to show that you are courageous cats. I have allowed Bertie and Camilla to join as they have shown courage on many occasions.'

'We have?' asked Bertie.

'Of course we have,' said Camilla loudly.

'When?' asked Tiger.

Bertie and Camilla looked at each other.

'Oh, hundreds of times,' said Camilla. 'Haven't we, Bertie?'

'Thousands.'

'Such as?' asked Tiger.

Bertie looked to Camilla for help.

'Such as… such as the time we chased a huge magpie,' said Camilla.

Tiger was impressed. 'That's very brave,' he said. 'Those magpies can be nasty.'

'So there you have it,' said Camilla. 'We are courageous cats.'

'Chased it up a big tree, we did,' said Bertie.

'Yes. That's enough,' said Camilla. 'So, as I said, we are courageous cats. End of conversation.'

'We chased it right to the very top,' added Bertie. 'It was only then that we realized we were far above the ground, balancing on the thinnest of branches. One wrong move and we would have fallen to certain death!'

Tiger gasped.

'We knew that we had to stay perfectly still,' said Bertie. 'But that was impossible!'

'Why?' asked Tiger. 'Why?'

'We were next to the magpie's nest! The magpie thought that we were trying to steal from it and let out a shriek to alert all the other magpies in the neighbourhood. From nowhere a flock of them swooped down, pecking and diving, diving and pecking.'

'What did you do?' asked Tiger, engrossed.

'What did we do?' Bertie asked himself. 'We fought them off! That's what we did!'

'All of them?'

'Yes. One of them nipped me and cut me, but I sent him packing with a swipe of my claws, didn't I, Camilla?'

'Yes, I'm sure you did, Bertie. So there you have it, we are courageous cats.'

'And just when I thought things couldn't get any worse, the wind began to blow,' added Bertie dramatically. 'And the tree started to sway to and fro, to and fro! In no time at all a gale was blowing, wasn't it, Camilla?'

Camilla didn't have time to speak before Bertie continued.

'We couldn't climb back down because of our injuries and we couldn't stay where we were because of the fierce wind. It was only a matter of time before we would be blown out of the tree and thrown to the ground!'

'And what happened?' asked Tiger eagerly.

'Yes, what did happen?' asked Camilla.
'Tell me Bertie, because I can't quite seem to remember.'

'I remember,' said Bertie excitedly. 'I just had enough energy to call for help. A neighbour heard my weak miaowing and sent for the fire brigade. They arrived with lights flashing and sirens sounding, and a fireman climbed the tree using a huge ladder and rescued us… just in the nick of time.'

'And were you all right?' asked Tiger, with great concern.

'We were taken to the vet's and he said we'd been very lucky. And very, very courageous.'

'Have you finished?' asked Clive.

Bertie nodded. 'Yes.'

'Good,' said Camilla.

'I won't tell them about the people from the TV company that came to make a film about it,' said Bertie.

Clive turned his attention to Tiger and Douglas.

'So I'm sure you will agree, Camilla and Bertie are courageous cats and for you two to join our club you must show your courage.'

Tiger suddenly became very scared. He had visions of being forced to climb huge trees or chase big magpies.

'You, Tiger, have already shown courage,' said Clive.

'I have?' asked Tiger.

'Yes. I think it takes great courage to speak up the way you did for your new friend. You were prepared to stand up against all of us for the sake of someone you believed had been treated unfairly. Courage can be shown in many different ways.'

Clive turned to Camilla and Bertie. 'I say Tiger is a Courageous Cat!'

'Courageous Cat!' shouted Camilla.

'Courageous Cat!' echoed Bertie.

'Is that it?' asked Tiger, his right ear starting to twitch. 'I'm in the club?'

'You certainly are,' said Clive. 'Well done.'

Clive looked at Douglas. 'So that just leaves you, Stumpy.'

'Please don't call him Stumpy,' said Tiger.

'It's all right,' said Douglas. 'Sticks and stones may break my bones, but names will never hurt me.'

Douglas decided that from now on he was going to stand up to Clive.

'So, what do I have to do to join the Courageous Cats' Club?' he asked.

'Simply show your courage,' said Clive smugly, and he stood on his hind legs and dug his claws into the tree trunk to sharpen them.

'How?' asked Douglas.

'Let me think.'

Clive dug his claws further into the tree. He was enjoying the attention of the others. They were hanging on his every word, wondering what daring deed he would force Douglas to perform.

Finally, Clive spoke: 'All you have to do, Stumpy... all you have to do to prove that you are a courageous cat, is run across old Mr Harding's lawn.'

There was a confused silence.

At last Camilla spoke: 'Is that all? Run across a lawn?'

'That's all,' said Clive.

'What's courageous about that?' asked Bertie.

'It's the biggest lawn in the neighbourhood,' said Tiger.

'So what?' snapped Camilla. 'I thought he was going to have to do something daring like steal a fish off Mr Wright's barbecue. That takes courage. We've all done that.'

'Calm down, calm down,' said Clive. 'Stumpy has just moved into his new home. It is up to us, his neighbours, to make him feel welcome. As leader of the Courageous Cats' Club, I say that all he has to do to become a member of our club is run across old Mr Harding's lawn. And that's final.'

'Hurray!' said Tiger. 'Come on, let's go and get it over with.'

'Not now,' said Clive. 'It's far too hot to be running around. We don't want Stumpy collapsing in the afternoon heat. It's a big lawn remember. We shall all meet again tomorrow morning when it's a little cooler.'

'What time?' asked Douglas.

'Oh, I don't know. Let's say about half past nine.'

With that Clive proclaimed the meeting closed and wandered off, winking at Tiger as he went.

'I still think you got off lightly, Stumpy,' said Camilla as she began to climb the apple tree to her favourite sunbathing spot.

'I'm off for a cat nap,' said Bertie. 'I'm quite exhausted.'

'Yes, fighting off all those magpies must have been very tiring,' said Camilla.

Bertie strolled towards his house and Camilla was soon snoozing in the sun.

Douglas whispered to Tiger, 'Is that really all I have to do? Run across a lawn?'

'Yes. Clive felt he had to make you do something so that he wouldn't lose face in front of the others,' explained Tiger. 'So he just picked something simple so that you can join the club and we can all get on with being friends. He likes you really.'

Douglas wasn't quite so sure.

7

A Terrible Accident

The next morning Douglas was up early and in old Mr Harding's garden before any of the others. It was a lovely garden, full of beautiful flowers, and there wasn't a weed in sight. The huge lawn was a lovely, rich, dark green – unlike most of the other lawns in the neighbourhood, which had turned brown from the scorching sun and lack of rain. A group of sparrows was twittering furiously in the silver birch tree that overlooked the garden. It was as if they had arrived early to get a good view and were now discussing the events to come with great excitement. Douglas stepped onto the grass, which was soft and springy under his paws.

'Only the best for you, Stumpy,' said Clive, who had crept up behind Douglas. 'I could

hardly ask you to run across your own lawn –
you might get lost in that overgrown dump.'

Clive laughed and Douglas forced a smile.

'Are you a good runner?' asked Clive.

'Not bad,' said Douglas.

He didn't really know. He was certainly as
fast as any other cat of his age.

Bertie and Camilla were next to arrive.

'I told you, Camilla,' said Bertie. 'This lawn
is gigantic.'

'It's not that big,' said Camilla. 'I don't see
what all the fuss is about.'

'I haven't missed anything, have I?' asked
Tiger excitedly, as he pushed his way through
a small gap under the fence.

'Right,' said Douglas. 'Everybody is here.
Let's get on with it.'

'Patience, patience,' said Clive. 'You run
across that lawn when I say so and not before.'

At that moment old Mr Harding came out
of the door at the back of the house.

'Quick, let's hide,' said Tiger.

'There's no need,' said Camilla. 'Old
Mr Harding is very short-sighted. He won't

see us. He can hardly see the nose on the end of his face even with those glasses he's wearing.'

'Shall I see if he wants to borrow mine?' said Bertie.

Camilla laughed and so Bertie cackled. Sure enough old Mr Harding walked straight past all the cats sitting at the edge of the lawn. He hadn't seen them.

He went into his garden shed and after a few minutes emerged pushing a big, old lawnmower.

'Oh no,' sighed Tiger. 'He's going to cut the grass. Now we'll have to call the whole thing off.'

'Old Mr Harding cuts his grass at half past nine every Tuesday,' said Clive with a grin. 'He's bang on time as usual.'

'Douglas can't run across the grass if that lawnmower is on it,' protested Tiger. 'It's dangerous.'

'It will spice things up a bit,' said Clive, with a mischievous look in his eyes.

'You didn't really think I would have asked him to simply scamper across an empty lawn, do you? What's courageous about that? No, this will test his courage. He will run across this lawn while it is being cut. Unless, of course, he wants to back out.' Clive stared at Douglas. 'All you have to do is run across the lawn when I say so. That was the agreement. Then you will have proved that you are a courageous cat.'

Mr Harding began to cut the grass with his old-fashioned lawnmower. The cats caught sight of the razor-sharp blades glinting in the early morning sunlight and watched the fine grass cuttings spraying from the mower.

'That thing would give you one heck of a haircut,' said Bertie.

'It will cut through anything in its path,' said Camilla, shivering as she watched the cold metal blades spinning round furiously.

'And as we know,' said Clive, 'Mr Harding is very short-sighted. He wouldn't see anything in his path until it was too late. If a cat were to run in front of that mower and not be quick enough on his feet, who knows what might happen?'

'Let's call the whole thing off,' said Tiger.

'Do you want to call it off, Stumpy?' asked Clive.

Douglas shook his head and slowly crouched

down and prepared himself. His head was practically level with the ground as he hunched up his long back legs to give himself a really good start.

'Just say the word and I'll run across the grass.'

Mr Harding had reached the far end of the lawn and was turning round to head back in their direction. Douglas knew that Clive would not give him much of a chance. He was going to have to run faster than he had ever run in his life to clear the path of that mower. He knew that if it hit him it would hurt him badly, possibly kill him, but he wasn't going to back out now.

'Be careful,' said Tiger.

'Shhh!' hissed Clive.

The mower was getting nearer and nearer.

'Wait… wait… wait…' whispered Clive.

Douglas was trembling. If that mower got any nearer it would be impossible to run across its path without being hit.

'Now!' shouted Clive.

Douglas sprang forward and ran for his life.

He darted across the lawn with his eyes fixed firmly on the fence opposite. As he passed in front of the lawnmower it was so close that he was sure that it had touched him.

He could hear the blades spinning and cutting and he could smell the fresh-cut grass as it sprayed into the air. Douglas crashed into the fence. He'd done it!

He lay on the ground gasping for breath. Mr Harding carried on mowing the lawn,

unaware of all the drama around him.

Douglas got to his feet, checked himself for any cuts and was relieved to find that he hadn't been hurt. Then he walked back towards the others, shaking off the bits of grass that had landed on his fur.

'Courageous Cat!' shouted Tiger.

Camilla and Bertie looked at Clive. None of them spoke.

'Courageous Cat!' Tiger shouted again, but still the others didn't join in.

Tiger persisted. 'He did it, Clive. He proved what courage he has.'

'It was easy,' sniffed Clive. 'Any cat could do it.'

'You couldn't do it,' said Douglas.

'Of course I could,' said Clive. 'I've done it hundreds of times just for fun. Anyway, *I* have nothing to prove.'

'Are you going to let Douglas join the Club?' asked Tiger.

'I might have to ask him to do something else,' said Clive.

'That's it,' said Douglas. 'I'm going home.'

'What's the matter, Stumpy?' asked Clive.

Douglas rounded on him. 'You said that courage can be shown in many ways, but you haven't got the courage to stand up and say that I did it fair and square!'

'Don't ever accuse me of being a coward!' shouted Clive. 'If you want to see courage watch this!' And Clive shot across the lawn.

Tiger looked away. Mr Harding was heading straight for Clive with the lawnmower, the flashing blades bearing down on him like teeth of steel. Bertie put his paws over his face. Camilla closed her eyes and screamed. Only Douglas watched as the lawnmower slammed into Clive and stopped with a jolt. There was a shriek of pain and an eerie silence fell over the whole neighbourhood. Even the birds were quiet. Old Mr Harding, shocked and confused, knelt down on the grass beside Clive. Clive didn't move.

8

Rain, Rain, Wash Away My Sorrow

Summer was all but over. Douglas sat under an old garden chair on the patio with the rain bouncing off the path in front of him. He hadn't seen any of the other cats since the accident and he was more sad and lonely than ever.

'Every cat in the neighbourhood hates me,' he said.

The gnome's head stared back at him, the rain running off the end of its broken beard.

'They'll never play with me, they'll never even speak to me. Every cat in London will know it's my fault that Clive is dead.'

A clap of thunder made him jump and the rain suddenly got much heavier. Douglas ran out into the garden. In no time at all he was soaking wet, but he didn't care. He ran round and round the garden shouting:

'Rain, rain, wash away my sorrow,
Please let the sun come out tomorrow!'

He ran faster and faster and shouted louder and louder:

'Rain, rain, wash away my sorrow,
Please let the sun come out tomorrow!'

Then he darted into the undergrowth and kept running until the ground was dry beneath his feet and there he collapsed, panting. When he had got his breath back, Douglas looked around and realized where he was. He was beneath the giant rhubarb plant where he had first met Tiger. Sure enough, one of the leaves moved to one side and a ginger face appeared.

'Hi,' said Tiger. 'I haven't seen you for ages. I thought you'd gone back to the Isle of Man.'

'I wish I had,' said Douglas.

Tiger emerged from the rhubarb.

'I hope you haven't been blaming yourself for what happened.'

'It was me who said Clive had no courage,'
said Douglas.

'Yes, but he should never have tried to show
off by running in front of that lawnmower.'

'I don't want to talk about it,' said Douglas.
'It's my fault he's dead and that's the end of it.'

'Dead?' Tiger laughed. 'Clive's not dead!'

'He's not?' asked Douglas in amazement.

'No. I saw him yesterday. I climbed up onto
his windowsill and peeped through the window.
He was lying in his box, fast asleep.'

'Is he all right?' asked Douglas urgently.

'I don't know. I think so. None of us has spoken to him properly. He's not been allowed out since the accident.'

'I'm so glad he's alive,' said Douglas. 'When do you think we'll be able to see him again?'

'I heard his owners saying that they might let him sit on the patio this afternoon, if it ever stops raining.'

Douglas smiled for the first time in many days.

'Listen,' he whispered.

Tiger pricked up his ears. 'I can't hear anything.'

'Exactly,' said Douglas. 'The rain has stopped.'

The two cats raced through the undergrowth towards Clive's house.

9

Visitors

By the time Douglas and Tiger reached Clive's garden the sun was trying to come out. Clive was curled up in a box on the back doorstep. Camilla and Bertie were sitting nearby. As Douglas approached, with Tiger by his side, he suddenly felt nervous.

'Do you mind if we join you?' he asked.

'Please do,' said Clive.

Clive's voice was weak and Douglas couldn't help but notice that he looked thin and tired. He seemed much older. For a while none of them knew what to say and the five cats sat in silence.

Finally Bertie spoke.

'I have something to tell you all,' he said quietly. 'I'm not a Courageous Cat.'

'Neither am I,' mumbled Camilla.

Bertie stared awkwardly at the ground, desperate not to make eye contact with the others.

'When I told you the story about the magpies at the top of the tree I got a bit carried away, I'm afraid. In fact, there weren't any magpies at all.'

'We climbed the tree to do a spot of sunbathing,' confessed Camilla. 'We fell asleep and a neighbour thought we were stuck and called the fire brigade.'

'We did get taken to the vet's,' said Bertie. 'But only because we were sunburned.'

Tiger laughed.

'So we're not quite as courageous as I led you to believe,' said Bertie with embarrassment. 'Sorry.'

Tiger laughed again. 'Maybe none of us is as courageous as we thought.'

'Oh, I don't know,' said Clive. He looked at Douglas. 'Our new friend here has shown a fair amount of courage, and I don't mean running in front of that lawnmower. He moved to a new home and tried to make new friends. We didn't make him feel particularly welcome, but he stuck at it. Good for him. Sometimes it takes courage just to be yourself. So, let's hear it for Douglas, the Courageous Cat!'

'Courageous Cat!' shouted the others.

Douglas wasn't sure what pleased him the most – the fact that he was one of the gang or the fact that Clive had used his proper name for the first time.

'Now I'm going inside, I feel a bit chilly,' said Clive. 'But before I go I want to show you all something.'

Clive stood up very slowly and carefully stepped out of his box.

'There,' he said. 'What have you all got to say about that?'

Camilla and Bertie and Tiger and Douglas gasped in horror. Clive had no tail. Just a stump.

'That lawnmower cut my tail so badly that the vet had to take it right off,' said Clive.

'I'm sorry,' said Douglas.

'It wasn't your fault,' said Clive. 'I guess I'm not as quick on my feet as I used to be. Anyway, thanks for coming to see me. I'm going inside

now and when I've gone you can all have a
good laugh.'

'We'd never do that, Clive,' said Camilla.

'Never in all our nine lives,' said Bertie.

Clive turned to go inside.

'You can even call me Stumpy,' he added
sadly, as he slowly walked to the door.

Douglas called after him. 'Hey!'

Clive stopped.

'Do you like Manx kippers?' asked Douglas.

Clive thought for a moment. 'I can't say that
I've ever had one. Why?'

'Some friends have sent some over from the Isle of Man and I'd like to share them with you all,' said Douglas. 'What do you say?'

'I'd like that,' said Clive, smiling.

'Me too,' said Camilla.

'Me three,' said Bertie.

'What's a kipper?' asked Tiger.

'A fish,' said Douglas. 'A smoked herring, to be precise.'

Tiger licked his lips and his right ear began to twitch.

10

Friends at Last

The following evening all the cats gathered in Douglas's garden for the first time. The sun was just going down and a light breeze brought with it the first faint smell of autumn.

'Here we are,' said Douglas, dragging the remains of four fish from behind the dustbin. 'These are Manx kippers,' he said proudly. 'I'd like you all to try them.'

Douglas watched as his friends started to eat. Clive was eating slowly and carefully, while Tiger was swallowing great lumps of kipper as if he'd never seen a fish before. Camilla was picking at hers, being very careful not to spill any bits on her lovely smooth coat, while Bertie ate a quick mouthful and then peered through his glasses to check that none of the

others had got more than him.

'Are Manx kippers different from ordinary kippers?' asked Tiger.

'Yes,' purred Camilla. 'They don't have tails,' she said, and laughed.

Bertie started to cackle, but then they remembered Clive's accident and were quiet.

'I suppose they're the same as any other kipper really,' said Douglas.

'I don't agree,' said Clive, as he picked a chunk of fish from a bone. 'They're much tastier than any ordinary kipper. You say they come from the Isle of Man? Why don't you tell us about the place?'

So Douglas sat in his new garden with his new friends and told them stories about the place where he was born. Tales of the enchanted island he came from. He told them about the little people who wear red caps and green jackets and who get up to all kinds of mischief and about the ruined castle that is haunted by a big black dog. And they all ate the tastiest fish in the whole world, Manx kippers.

The Beast of the Night

Contents

1

⁝

Dramatic News

Tiger felt a tug on the end of his fishing line. He
eagerly pulled another goldfish from the pond
and plopped it into the jam jar by his side. It
was the third one he had caught and he knew
there was only one more left. He licked his lips
at the thought of a tasty supper and dangled
his fishing line into the water for the last time.

Suddenly Tiger found that he was being
pulled towards the edge of the pond! He wedged
his back paws between two big pebbles to stop
himself from being dragged into the water.

'So you want to make a fight of it, do you?'
he said.

He took a big breath and pulled on the fishing
line as hard as he could. Two big ears came out
of the water. Tiger watched in terror as they

were followed by a pair of dark, evil eyes, a flat, wet nose and a huge pair of pointed, shiny teeth. It wasn't a fish on the end of the line, it was Fang, the big dog from Number 12.

Fang roared and lunged out of the water. Tiger dropped his fishing line and turned to run away, but he was too slow! Fang pounced on top of the little cat and swallowed him in one gulp!

'Tiger! Tiger!'

Somebody was calling his name.

'Tiger! Tiger, wake up!'

Somebody was shaking him. Tiger opened his eyes and was greeted by the smiling face of his friend Douglas.

'Are you all right, Tiger? You've been making some very strange noises in your sleep.'

'I was having a bad dream,' said Tiger. 'At least, I hope it was a dream.'

Tiger looked nervously around the garden and was relieved to see that there was no sign of Fang. He peered into the pond and saw the four goldfish just beneath the surface of the water. Tiger felt sure that they were laughing at him.

The fish lived in Douglas's garden. It was one of the nicest in the neighbourhood, but it hadn't always been like that. When Douglas and his owner, Sarah, moved into their new house, the garden was very scruffy and overgrown.

During the spring, Sarah had spent many hours pulling up weeds and cutting back bushes and plants. While she was doing this she had discovered an old, dried-out pond. She cleared it out, filled it with water and bought the four little goldfish. Then Sarah placed some pebbles and seashells all around the pond, together with little stone sailors and pirates and a small wooden lighthouse. She put some decking under the huge fir tree, and on it she put a coiled rope, a small rusty anchor and a big, old crab basket. Now every time Sarah and Douglas went into their beautiful garden, they were reminded of the seaside where they had both been born.

The crab basket had become a favourite sunbathing spot for all the local cats, especially Tiger.

'You always fall asleep when you sit on that basket,' said Douglas.

'It's so comfortable,' said Tiger. 'What is it exactly?'

'It was used to catch crabs.'

'How?'

'It's heavy so that it sinks to the bottom of the sea. When the crabs crawl inside they get tangled up in the netting and can't escape.'

Tiger hopped down from the basket and stuck his nose inside the large flap at the end and gazed at the maze of fine netting inside.

'Be careful,' said Douglas. 'If you get stuck in there you might never be able to get out.'

Just then there was a thud against the garden fence. Clive had arrived. This was followed a few seconds later by another thud, which was Bertie. The two cats clambered onto the top of the fence, dropped to the ground and ran across the lawn towards the others.

'Have you heard the news?' gasped Clive when he reached Douglas and Tiger. 'Mr Wright's dustbin was pushed over during the night!'

Bertie, who was very fat, was so short of breath he could only manage one word: 'Again!'

'Rubbish has been scattered all around his garden,' continued Clive excitedly.

'Again!' wheezed Bertie.

'And Mr Wright said that if he catches the cat who did it, he'll have him taken away and put in a cats' home!'

Douglas shuddered at the thought. 'Who do you think is to blame?' he asked.

'I don't know,' said Clive. 'Have you seen any strange cats in the neighbourhood?'

'No,' said Douglas. 'But somebody or something was moving around in my garden in the middle of the night. I heard them scraping around near the shed.'

'I've heard some strange noises over the last few nights as well,' said Bertie. 'Like a whining and screaming. Very spooky it was.'

'I think this calls for an investigation,' said Clive. 'All Courageous Cats to meet at midnight. Usual place.'

'Midnight?' Bertie didn't like the idea of having to stay up so late.

'That's the best time to watch out for the mystery intruder,' said Clive. 'I'll let Camilla know. She won't want to miss out on the excitement.'

'I won't be able to come,' said Tiger quietly.

'Why not?' asked Clive.

'I'm not allowed out late at night.'

'But…' began Clive.

He paused as suddenly Tiger jumped off the decking, ran across the lawn and disappeared under the hedge at the bottom of the garden.

'I think we've scared him,' said Douglas.

'Perhaps he's right to be scared,' said Clive.

'What do you mean?' asked Bertie.

'We don't know who or what is creeping about in the darkness,' said Clive mysteriously. 'But tonight we shall find out.'

2

A Midnight Meeting

It was a perfect night for an investigation, dry
and clear with plenty of light from the moon.
Clive was the first to arrive beneath the apple
tree in Bertie's back garden. Like most cats,
Clive loved to go out at night. He enjoyed the
stillness and the quiet when most of the humans
had gone to bed and stopped making all their
noise. Now there were no loud televisions or
thumping music systems.

Nobody was shouting and there was hardly
any traffic. As Clive sharpened his claws on the
tree trunk, he counted the crisp, clear chimes of
the town hall clock in the distance. On the fifth
stroke, Douglas ran across the moonlit lawn.
Seven strokes later, Bertie came out of his house
and ambled towards the apple tree.

'Where's Camilla?' asked Douglas.

'In bed, if she's got any sense,' said Bertie, with a yawn.

Clive looked up into the branches above his head to check that there wasn't a creamy shape hiding in the darkness.

'If she's not here in a couple of minutes we'll start without her.'

'What are we going to do if we meet the mysterious intruder?' asked Douglas.

'Hide,' said Bertie. 'If you think that I'm going to…'

'Shhh!' hissed Clive.

The three cats pricked up their ears and listened carefully. They could hear a faint tinkling sound some way off. The cats gave each other a puzzled look. There it was again, but this time it was a little louder.

'What is it?' whispered Douglas.

'I don't know,' said Clive. 'But it's heading this way. Quickly, up the tree.'

The three cats raced up the thin trunk and perched on the branches, watching and listening. The tinkling sound was growing

louder and louder and whatever was making it
was getting nearer and nearer. There was a
rustle in the bushes nearby and the three cats
watched as a figure came out of the shadows.
It was Camilla. Around her neck was a collar
with a small bell. Clive let out a huge laugh,
dropped from the tree and went to have a
closer look.

'Who's a pretty girl, then?'

'Shut up,' hissed Camilla.

She liked to think of herself as the most

beautiful cat in London, and she knew that the bell was ruining her image.

'I've heard of cows wearing bells, but not cats!' sniggered Clive.

Camilla flashed her claws and took a swipe at Clive, who just managed to dodge out of the way.

'There's no time for fighting,' said Bertie, as he climbed down the tree trunk. 'We're already late. Camilla, you should have let us know that you weren't going to be here on time.'

'How was I supposed to do that?'

'You could have given us a ring!'

Bertie let out a huge cackle of laughter, collapsed on the ground, rolled onto his back and waved his paws in the air. Camilla pounced on top of him and Bertie shrieked, more out of surprise than pain. No sooner had Camilla pinned Bertie to the ground than Clive charged into her, sending her flying through the air.

Camilla scrambled to her feet, her bell ringing furiously, and was about to launch herself at Clive when Douglas dropped from the tree and landed between them.

'We're here on a secret mission and you're

all making enough noise to wake the whole neighbourhood,' he said.

'He started it,' snapped Camilla.

'You started it,' shouted Clive.

'It doesn't matter who started it,' said Douglas. 'Come on, let's go to my garden. That's where I heard the intruder last night.'

The four cats moved silently through the undergrowth – silently, that is, except for the tinkling of the little bell.

'Can't you keep that thing quiet?' said Clive.

Camilla said nothing and tried walking on the tips of her paws, but it didn't make any difference. She crouched down and tried crawling along the ground, but still the tinkle-tinkle rang through the air.

'This is no good,' said Clive. 'How can we expect to creep up on the mystery intruder with that bell announcing our every move? We'll have to lie low and keep a lookout from here.'

The cats slipped into the bushes and lay down. Finally the bell was silent. They watched and listened, but the only thing they saw and heard was a hedgehog rummaging in some leaves as he looked for a midnight feast.

'Why has your owner given you a bell?' whispered Douglas.

'I gave her a present and so she gave me this in return,' whispered Camilla.

'What did you give her?'

'A dead bird. I wanted to show her how much I love her. I crept into her bedroom while she was asleep and put the bird on her pillow so that it would be the first thing she saw when she woke up.'

'Was she pleased?'

'She started screaming and running round the bedroom. Then she locked me in the kitchen while she went to the pet shop and bought me this.'

'I don't understand humans,' said Douglas, shaking his head.

'It's so that I won't be able to catch any more birds. When they hear the bell they fly away. That's the idea, but give me a few days and I'll be able to move around without making a sound, you'll see.'

'Shh!' said Clive urgently.

Camilla and Douglas stopped talking and they too could hear a strange, low rumbling noise.

'Nobody move,' whispered Clive. He looked at Camilla and the bell around her neck. 'Especially you!'

There was no sign of anyone or anything in the garden, but the rumbling sound was still there. The cats hardly dared to breathe. After a few terrified minutes, Clive broke the silence.

'Whatever it is, it's pretty close,' he whispered.

'Very close,' agreed Douglas. 'It's right next to you.'

Clive looked round nervously. Curled up on the ground, fast asleep, was Bertie, snoring loudly. Clive gave him a prod and the rumbling stopped.

'Have I missed anything?' asked Bertie wearily. 'Apart from my bed?'

'If it's not her ringing, it's you rumbling!' yelled Clive. 'We're never going to solve this mystery if we can't keep quiet!' he shouted.

'Does that mean we can go home?' asked Bertie hopefully.

'Yes!'

Clive jumped to his feet and stomped off towards his house and the others immediately headed for their own homes. As Douglas padded through the undergrowth he chuckled to himself. Courageous Cats, he thought. Scared by a little bell and then spooked by Bertie's snoring.

Then he heard it! Something was moving about in the darkness. Slowly and quietly Douglas sank to the ground and peered all around. He couldn't see anything, but he could tell that something was very close by. Worse still, he could sense that it was a lot bigger than him. Douglas tried to stay as quiet as possible, but his heart was thumping so loudly he was scared that it would give him away.

Suddenly the night air was split with a terrifying scream. It was like the screaming of a baby, but not a human baby... this sound was unlike anything Douglas had ever heard before. A chill ran down his spine and he felt his fur bristle with fear.

Douglas ran for his life.

3
∴
Clues

The bone was sticking out of the soil in
Douglas's garden.

'It's a chicken drumstick,' said Bertie.

'And all the meat has been ripped off it,'
added Clive.

'By what?' asked Camilla, trying her best not
to sound frightened.

'Not a cat,' said Douglas. 'A cat would never
bury its food.'

The four cats were continuing their
investigation in the daylight. Clive paced round
and round the bone, obviously enjoying playing
cat detective.

'What exactly did you see last night,
Douglas?'

'I've already told you, I didn't *see* anything.'

'What did you hear?'

For the fifth time that morning Douglas told the others about the creature that he had heard moving about in the darkness.

'Do you think it was too big to be a cat?'

'Yes, I think so.'

'Then I have an announcement to make,' said Clive dramatically. 'As leader of this investigation, I am convinced that the beast of the night is...'

'What's going on?' Tiger squeezed through a gap under the fence.

'Shh!' said Camilla. 'Clive is about to reveal the identity of the beast of the night!'

Tiger gulped.

'As I was saying,' said Clive, 'I am convinced that the beast of the night is... not a cat.'

'We don't want to know what it isn't!' exclaimed Camilla. 'We want to know what it is!'

'I haven't worked that out yet,' said Clive.

'Look at this!' Douglas had found another clue on the decking under the fir tree. The others ran towards him and looked at the tiny pieces of bone dotted all around the crab basket.

'More chicken drumstick,' said Clive.

'That's not chicken bone,' said Bertie.

Bertie was the best fed cat in the neighbourhood and the others respected his opinion on all things to do with food.

'It's lamb.'

'And there's not much of it left,' said Camilla.

'The rest of the bone has probably been eaten by the beast,' said Clive. 'Crunched into tiny pieces and swallowed.'

'And look at this!' shouted Douglas.

'Let me see, let me see,' said Clive, pushing past the others.

A trail of paw prints led into the bushes.

'I was right,' said Clive. 'The beast is definitely not a cat. It has four paws like us, but these prints are far too big to have been made by one of our kind.'

'So what is it then?' asked Camilla impatiently.

'That is what we are about to find out,' answered Clive. 'If we follow the trail of paw prints, it will lead us to the beast.'

'No!' shouted Tiger. 'We mustn't do that.'

'There's no need to be scared,' said Clive. 'There are five of us. Five Courageous Cats

against one beast. No contest. And when we
follow the trail we will know what sort of
creature it is.'

'It's a dog!' shouted Tiger.

The others were stunned by this sudden
outburst.

'How can you be so sure?' asked Bertie.

'Because I've seen it! I know who it is! It's Fang!'

'Fang?' said Camilla. 'The dog from Number 12?'

'That's right,' said Tiger. 'He came to my house last night. The kitchen door was open and he sneaked inside and stole a bone from the table. It was a big lamb bone. Then he brought it here.'

'How do you know?' asked Clive.

'I followed him.'

The others gasped in amazement.

'That was very courageous of you,' said Clive. 'But I thought you weren't allowed out at night.'

'I'm not, but... I wanted to see what he was up to. I followed him here and watched him smash the bone into tiny pieces with his big sharp teeth. Then he must have stolen the chicken drumstick from somebody else's house.'

'Or somebody else's dustbin,' said Clive.

'That's right!' exclaimed Tiger. 'Fang is the one who's been pushing over the bins and making a mess of the gardens.'

'Why didn't you tell us all this earlier?' asked Douglas. 'Why didn't you tell us that it was Fang?'

'Because… because I wanted Clive to solve the mystery.'

'That's very kind of you, Tiger,' said Clive. 'But I already had. I always suspected it was a dog, I just wasn't sure which one.'

'So that horrible dog has been messing up the gardens and we cats have been getting the blame,' said Camilla.

'We're not going to let him get away with this,' said Clive firmly. 'Come on everybody, follow me to Number 12.'

'I don't think we should do that,' said Tiger nervously. 'He'll attack us.'

Clive was already heading out of the garden. Tiger continued his protest as he followed.

'He's vicious… he might eat us…'

As Tiger's voice trailed off in the distance, Bertie and Camilla gave each other a worried look.

'I'm not so sure this is a good idea,' said Camilla.

'Neither am I,' agreed Bertie.

'We can't let them go on their own,' said Douglas. 'Besides, I think we might be in for a surprise when we finally get to meet the beast.'

'Why?' asked Camilla. 'What do you mean?'

Douglas took another look at the paw prints.

'Clive was right when he said these prints weren't made by a cat. But I've got a funny feeling that they weren't made by a dog either!'

4

Ferocious Fang

Clive scrambled silently up the garage wall at Number 12 and looked down into the yard below. Lying on the ground was Fang, fast asleep. Clive nodded to Douglas, who joined him on the garage roof. Bertie was next up, followed by Tiger, who stared uneasily at the big dog.

'I told you he was horrible,' Tiger whispered. 'You can tell that he's nasty just by looking at him.'

Fang wasn't the most handsome dog in the world. His face was squashed and wrinkled like an old party balloon. He had a flat nose and big sagging cheeks.

Right now saliva was dribbling from his mouth and making a small puddle on the floor.

'Why would anybody want to keep that as a pet?' whispered Bertie.

'He's not even a good guard dog,' added Clive quietly. 'He hasn't heard us climb up here.'

Camilla was still sitting in the garden below.

'Is it safe?' she asked.

'Of course it is,' said Clive. 'Don't be such a scaredy cat.'

Camilla scrambled up onto the garage roof. As she did so, the bell on her collar tinkled. It was the slightest of sounds, but enough to wake the huge dog. Fang lunged at the garage wall, barking wildly, and the five cats nearly jumped out of their skin. There was no way Fang could reach them, but that didn't stop him from going absolutely crazy.

'Let's get out of here!' yelled Tiger.

'No, no,' shouted Clive. 'Once the silly creature realizes that he can't reach us, he'll calm down.'

Barking loudly, the big dog paced up and down the yard with his eyes fixed on the cats above for five more minutes. Then finally, Fang lay on the ground and was quiet.

'I am the leader of the Courageous Cats' Club,' Clive announced formally.

'Having carried out an investigation, I hereby declare that you, Fang the dog, have been found guilty of pushing over dustbins and stealing food.'

'I think we should give him a chance to say something before we decide that he's guilty,' interrupted Douglas. 'What if it wasn't him?'

'Of course it was him,' said Clive. 'He was seen stealing a bone and eating it.'

'He does look like a thief,' said Camilla.

'And a thug,' added Bertie.

Clive spoke to the big dog again.

'We have been getting the blame for your bad behaviour. If you don't stop it at once we will sneak into your house and scratch the furniture, and you will get the blame for it. Then you will be sent to the dogs' home where you belong.'

'I still think we should give him a chance to speak,' said Douglas.

'Oh, very well,' said Clive reluctantly. 'Fang, do you admit to being the beast of the night?'

Fang shook his head.

'He's bound to say that,' said Tiger. 'Come on, let's go.'

Douglas was determined to give Fang a chance.

'Can you prove that you are *not* the beast of the night?'

Much to the cats' surprise, Fang nodded his head.

'How?' asked Clive. 'How can you prove that

you haven't been pushing over the dustbins? How can you prove that you didn't steal the bone and eat it?'

Fang opened his mouth and the cats waited for him to say something, but he remained silent. The huge dog simply sat there with his mouth wide open.

'What's the matter with him?' asked Camilla, confused.

'He's proving that he's not guilty,' said Douglas. 'Don't you see?'

'All I can see is a big empty mouth,' said Bertie.

'Exactly. Totally empty. Fang hasn't got any teeth!'

Douglas was right. There wasn't one tooth in the big dog's mouth.

'What happened to your teeth?' asked Clive.

Fang spoke for the first time.

'They had to be taken out last year,' he said with a deep, gruff voice.

'How do you eat?' asked Douglas.

'I'm only allowed soft foods. Even my dog biscuits have to be soaked in warm milk before I can eat them.'

'So you wouldn't be able to eat a bone?' asked Douglas. 'Even if you wanted to?'

Fang shook his head.

'No, I can't eat bones any more. So you see, there is no way that I could be the beast of the night.'

Just then a big tear rolled down one of Fang's cheeks and dropped onto the ground.

'This always happens to me,' he said sadly. 'Everybody takes one look at me and thinks I'm a troublemaker. You all thought I was a thug and a thief, but you don't even know me.'

The cats were very embarrassed and didn't know what to say.

Fang continued. 'And just because I bark a lot everybody thinks I'm nasty, but it's just my way of saying hello.'

'We made a mistake,' said Douglas. 'And we're sorry.' He turned to the other cats. 'Aren't we?'

Clive, Bertie and Camilla nodded their heads.

'We realize now that you're not a bad dog,' said Douglas.

'Does that mean you'll be my friends?' asked Fang quietly.

Douglas was so shocked by the question that he was lost for words. He looked to the others for help, but they were equally confused. None of them had ever been friends with a dog before.

'All I've ever wanted is to have some friends,' continued Fang. 'But none of the dogs round here will have anything to do with me. Even humans cross the road to avoid me.'

After an awkward silence, Douglas spoke again.

'We'd love to be your friends,' he said.

He turned to the other cats. 'Wouldn't we?'

Clive, Bertie and Camilla couldn't think of a reason to say no, so they nodded their heads. Fang was delighted, and he wagged his tail so hard that the cats thought it was going to fly off.

It was then that Clive noticed that Tiger was crying.

'I think you've got some explaining to do,' said Clive gently. 'Why did you say that you had seen Fang eating that bone?'

Tiger didn't answer.

'It's all right,' said Douglas. 'You can tell us.'

'I can't,' sobbed Tiger.

'What do you mean, you can't?'

'The beast said... the beast said that if I ever told anybody then it would eat me for its supper.'

'You really have seen the beast?' asked Bertie, astonished.

Tiger nodded. 'Many times.'

'Are you telling the truth?' asked Clive sternly.

'Yes, honestly.'

The cats bombarded Tiger with questions.

'Who is it?'

'What is it?'

'Where did you see it?'

'I can't tell you,' insisted Tiger.

'Yes, you can,' said Douglas. 'We're your friends. If you're in trouble we'll help you.'

Tiger took several deep breaths and began his story.

'For the last few weeks Mrs Russell at Number 4 has left some bits of boiled ham on the patio. I went there last Tuesday evening, ate the ham as usual, then headed for home. It was just going dark and as I was walking through the garden I heard something moving about in the bushes. I didn't know what it was and I was frightened, so I started to run. Suddenly the beast was there! Standing in front of me!'

'A dog? A cat?' asked Clive urgently.

'No. I've never seen a creature like this before. It's twice as big as any of us with glowing green eyes and big, white teeth.'

The cats gasped and Fang got to his feet and moved closer so that he could hear better.

'It accused me of stealing its food. I said the ham was for me, but the beast said I was a liar as well as a thief and that as a punishment I had to bring it some food every night. The first night I took some meat from my bowl, but the beast wanted more. That's when I started stealing. It was me who stole the lamb bone. And the chicken drumstick. I had to.'

Tiger began to cry again.

'And now I've told you… and now I've told you…'

'It's all right,' said Douglas. 'You've done the

right thing by telling us. This beast is a bully, and the best way to beat a bully is to tell somebody about it. We'll do everything we can to help you.'

'We certainly will,' said Clive. 'All Courageous Cats must meet at midnight in Douglas's garden. And I want you all to bring some food for the beast.'

The others looked at him with a mixture of confusion and terror.

'Don't worry,' said Clive. 'I have a plan.'

The others immediately began to worry.

5

Trapped!

It was a very dark night. The moon was doing its best to peep out from behind the thick clouds, but it wasn't having much luck. In the blackness the five cats gathered on the decking under the fir tree.

'Why are we meeting in my garden?' asked Douglas.

'You'll see,' said Clive.

'But the beast told me to meet him in the garden at Number 20,' said Tiger nervously.

'Go and meet the beast as planned,' said Clive. 'Tell him that you've got so much food for him that you simply can't carry it all. That should make him come back here with you.'

'But if he sees all of you he'll know that…'

'Don't worry, Tiger, we'll all be hiding,' said Clive gently.

'We certainly will,' added Camilla.

The cats watched as Tiger bravely set off to meet the beast.

'Now, what food did you bring?' asked Clive. 'I have brought two chips which I found in the street.'

'I've brought a piece of meat from my dinner,' said Douglas.

'Well done,' said Clive. 'What about you, Camilla?'

'I've got a chicken bone. I found it in an old takeaway box.'

'Excellent. We know that the beast is fond of chicken. Bertie, what have you got for us?'

'I managed to get a piece of the finest tuna fish,' said Bertie.

'Well done. Let's have it then.'

'But I had an accident on the way here.'

'What kind of accident?'

'I swallowed it. Sorry.'

Just then there was movement in the bushes. Clive hastily arranged the scraps of food all around the wooden decking.

'What are you doing?' whispered Douglas.

'All part of my plan,' said Clive quietly. 'Now let's get out of here.'

Clive darted up the fir tree, followed by Douglas. Camilla and Bertie had already found a safe spot on a high branch. They all held their breath as Tiger walked onto the decking below. Behind him was the beast of the night.

Tiger was right. It was twice as big as he was. It had dark fur with a white flash down each side of its long snout. Its huge tail was also dark, apart from the very tip, which looked as if it had been dipped in a tin of white paint. It had pointed ears, glowing green eyes and brilliant white teeth that glistened when it spoke.

'You'd better have some tasty treats for me or I'll rip your tail off!' spat the beast.

High in the tree Camilla began to shake with fear, making her bell ring. So Bertie, who was sitting next to her, did the first thing that came into his head. He opened his mouth and closed it around the little bell so that the sound could hardly be heard. The beast looked up into the tree.

'What was that noise?'

'I didn't hear anything,' said Tiger. 'Look, I brought some chips for you,' he added, desperately trying to distract the beast.

The beast stared up into the dark branches.

'I hope you haven't told anybody about our little arrangement.'

'No, of course not,' said Tiger.

'Because you know what will happen if you do.'

Tiger nodded. 'You'll eat me for your supper,' he mumbled.

'Exactly.'

The beast pounced on one of the chips and gobbled it up.

'Is that it?'

'No, there's lots more food,' said Tiger eagerly. 'Look, here's another chip.'

The beast trotted across the decking, inspected the chip, then snapped it up and ate it.

'And here's a bone for you.'

The beast sniffed his way towards the chicken bone, picked it up, crunched it into tiny pieces and swallowed the lot.

'And there's a piece of meat for you,' said Tiger.

The final piece of food was inside the crab basket. The beast used one of his paws to lift the flap at the end of the basket and then poked his long snout inside, but he couldn't quite reach the lump of meat. He stretched out a front leg and tried to drag the meat towards him with his paw, but again he couldn't quite get hold of it. The beast licked his lips and slowly eased himself into the basket. He shuffled along on his belly until his whole body was inside.

As the beast gobbled up the last tasty treat, Clive dropped from the tree and slammed the basket shut. He quickly picked up a stick in his mouth and used it to fasten the basket so that the beast couldn't get out. Suddenly it was as if the basket had a life of its own. It lifted from the decking and then smashed down again as the beast struggled to get free. Up and down, up and down, hammering against the wooden surface. The cats watched in amazement as the basket stood on one end and bounced across the decking before thumping down again and rolling over and over.

At last the basket stopped moving as the beast, tangled in the fine netting, collapsed, exhausted. Now the only sound to be heard was a faint tinkling high up in the tree. Bertie had opened his mouth and let go of the bell, and Camilla was shaking so much that the tinkle-tinkle rang out across the gardens.

Douglas and Bertie joined Clive and Tiger on the decking and together they slowly approached the basket. They peered cautiously through the netting to get a proper look at their prisoner.

'Have any of you ever seen such a creature before?' asked Douglas.

'No,' said Clive.

'I have,' said Bertie. 'On TV. I can safely say that the beast of the night is a fox.'

Clive laughed. 'A fox? This is the middle of London. What would a fox be doing round here?'

'He must be an urban fox,' said Bertie. 'They live in the city.'

Suddenly the beast let out an ear-piercing scream. All the cats jumped and Camilla's bell, which had been silent for a few seconds, started to ring again. The fox began to whine and the chilling sound made the cats feel very uncomfortable.

'I think we should move on to the second part of your plan,' said Douglas.

Clive didn't say anything.

'You do have a second part to your plan, don't you?'

'I thought of the first part,' said Clive. 'Somebody else can think of the second. Do I have to do everything round here?'

'Oh great!' said Bertie. 'We've got ourselves a beast in a basket and we've no idea what to do next!'

'I think we should let him go,' said Douglas.

'Let him go?' snapped Clive. 'Why would we want to do that?'

'Because he's only a baby. He's not a full-grown fox, he's a fox cub.'

'How do you know?' asked Bertie.

'Because he's so small.'

'He looks pretty big to me,' said Tiger.

'If you think he's big, wait until you see his mum and dad,' said Douglas. 'They're huge.'

'How do you know?' asked Clive.

'They're standing behind you.'

116

Clive was frozen to the spot. If this was a joke, it wasn't very funny. If it wasn't a joke, it was even less so. Clive turned around ever so slowly. Standing behind him were two snarling foxes who were both three times his size.

6

A Surprise in the Shadows

Clive made a dash for the fir tree. He didn't
know if foxes could climb trees, but he was
prepared to take the risk. Tiger and Douglas
followed in a flash, but Bertie was too slow. As
he started to scramble up the tree, one of the big
foxes grabbed him by the tail and dragged him,
shrieking, to the ground. Bertie was shaking
with fear as the fox pinned him down with his
front paws and leaned into his face.

'You need to lose some weight,' it said.

Bertie was inches from the huge teeth of
the fox and could smell its stinking breath.
He closed his eyes and waited... and waited...
but nothing happened. The fox was glancing

nervously towards the bushes, as if it could sense there was another creature out there in the darkness. There was. A huge dark figure walked slowly out of the shadows, stood on the edge of the decking and let out a deep, menacing growl. It was Fang! The two foxes replied with vicious snarls and Bertie gave out a shrill shriek. This prompted the other cats into high-pitched wailing, which was topped only by the whining of the fox cub. The night air was filled with an ear-piercing chorus of animal sounds, accompanied by the ringing of Camilla's bell.

'Stop it!' Tiger tried to quieten the din, but nobody could hear him.

'Stop it, stop it, stop it!' he shouted, at the top of his voice.

Fang stopped growling, the foxes stopped snarling, Bertie stopped shrieking, the cats stopped wailing, the cub stopped whining and the bell stopped ringing. Tiger turned to all the cats.

'When I told you that the fox cub was bullying me you said you would help me. But now everybody is going to start fighting. How will *that* help?'

'You're right,' said Douglas quietly. 'We've been no help at all. The fox cub was picking on you, so we picked on him. We should be ashamed of ourselves.'

The fox cub's dad had been listening carefully and he let go of Bertie. The terrified cat struggled to his feet and shot up the tree as fast as he could. Keeping a wary eye on Fang, the fox walked over to the crab basket and peered inside at the cub.

'Is this true? Have you been bullying the little cat?'

'He took some food that was meant for me. He...'

'That's no excuse for bullying. Apologize, please.'

'Sorry,' mumbled the fox cub.

The fox cub's dad looked up into the tree and called out to the cats. 'And I'm sorry too. This won't happen again.'

He was about to pull the stick from the basket to release the cub, but stopped when Fang began to growl again.

'I'm going to release my son,' explained

the fox. 'The little cat will be safe.'

'What about the rest of us?' shouted Bertie, who was still shaking.

'None of you will be harmed,' said the fox.

'How do we know that?' asked Clive from the safety of a high branch. 'How do we know we can trust you?'

'You don't,' said the fox. 'Just as we don't know that we can trust this dog not to harm us.' He turned to Fang. 'All we can do is give our word. That will have to be enough. Do you agree?'

Fang nodded his head, so the fox pulled the stick from the basket. The cub scrambled out of the trap and ran straight to his mum's side.

The fox called into the tree once again. 'It seems that all this trouble was caused by food.'

'He took some scraps that were meant for me,' said the cub.

'No, they were for me,' shouted Tiger.

'Please, don't argue,' said Douglas. 'We need to find a way to solve this problem calmly and peacefully.'

'There isn't a problem,' said Camilla, who was

feeling a little more brave now Fang had arrived on the scene. 'If one of the humans left some food out it was obviously meant for us cats.'

The fox cub's mum spoke for the first time. 'We're entitled to that food just as much as you are.'

'No, you're not,' said Camilla.

'This is getting us nowhere,' said the fox cub's dad. 'Perhaps we should all go home and calm down. Maybe we can get together another

time and try and sort things out.'

'I hope you're not planning to organize a meeting,' said Clive.

'I just thought that...'

'*I* organize all the meetings round here. As it happens, I was just about to suggest we all meet here again at midnight tomorrow.'

'Why does everything have to happen in the middle of the night?' asked Bertie.

'And why does there have to be so much talking?' asked Tiger.

'Talking is a better way of solving a problem than fighting,' said Douglas.

'I agree,' said the fox. 'We'll meet here at midnight tomorrow.'

The fox nodded a goodnight to Fang and then led his family into the bushes. The cats watched the white tips of the foxes' tails bobbing through the darkness until they disappeared.

'We're not really going to meet them, are we?' whispered Camilla. 'What if it's a trick? What if there are more foxes out there? What if...'

'We've just agreed that we're going to trust each other,' said Douglas. 'The fox gave his word that we will be safe and Fang gave his word that he won't harm the foxes. And I think we should all say a big thank you to Fang. If he hadn't come along, I dread to think what might have happened.'

'Thank you, Fang,' said Clive.

'Yes, thanks for helping us,' added Bertie.

'That's what friends are for,' said the big dog, wagging his tail.

'How did you know we needed help?' asked Tiger.

'I heard an alarm bell,' said Fang.

The cats turned and looked at Camilla.

'Er… yes, that was me,' she said. 'Good idea of mine, wasn't it? Shaking so that my bell would ring.'

One by one the others began to laugh.

'What's so funny?' asked Camilla. 'I *was* raising the alarm, honestly.'

7

The Agreement

'I declare this meeting open,' said Clive, who had put himself in charge as usual.

He was sitting on top of the crab basket, which gave him a feeling of superiority. (It also meant that he could be first up the tree if it all turned nasty.) Sitting around him in the darkness were all the other members of the Courageous Cats' Club. On the other side of the decking was the fox cub with his mum and dad. Sitting between the two groups was Fang, listening carefully like an old judge.

'We have to decide who is entitled to eat the scraps of food put out by the humans,' announced Clive.

'*We* are,' said Camilla. 'We live here.'

'We live here too,' said the fox cub's dad.

'We've made a den underneath the shed.'

'We're your new neighbours,' said the fox cub's mum politely.

Clive, Camilla and Bertie looked at each other. They didn't seem very keen on their new neighbours.

'That doesn't mean that you can help yourself to food that's been left out for us,' said Camilla.

'It's not all meant for you,' said the cub. 'One of the humans leaves scraps for us.'

'And we're extremely grateful,' said the cub's mum. 'It's much nicer than what we usually eat. Normally we have to survive on worms or insects or berries or even rubbish from a dustbin.'

'So you admit it!' exclaimed Clive. 'It is you foxes who have been raiding the dustbins and making a mess of people's gardens.'

'And we've been getting the blame,' said Bertie.

'I think it's disgusting,' said Camilla. 'You wouldn't catch any of us scraping around in smelly rubbish.' She began to lick her coat as if she'd become dirty at the thought of it. 'And you certainly wouldn't find us living under a filthy old shed.'

'Our ways are different from yours,' said the cub's dad. 'We move around from one place to another and make a home wherever we can. We spend all our time out of doors and so we have to scrape around to find our food.'

'Very strange behaviour,' mumbled Bertie.

'It might seem strange to you,' said the cub's mum, 'but your ways seem strange to us. We've peered through your windows after dark. We've seen you having your meals served in a little bowl, sleeping on top of a radiator, being kissed and cuddled by humans. Very strange indeed.'

Camilla licked a paw and wiped it over her face. 'If you don't like our behaviour why don't you go back to wherever it is you came from?'

'Why are you here anyway?' asked Tiger. 'I thought foxes lived in the countryside.'

'Some do,' said the cub's dad. 'But over the years, humans have made the countryside smaller and smaller. They have built houses and roads and destroyed many woods and fields. Many of us foxes have been driven out of our homes and we've had to learn to live in towns. Some humans welcome us and leave us scraps of food, but others see us as pests.'

'We were hoping that you would make us feel welcome,' said the cub's mum.

'Why should we?' asked Clive. 'You steal our food and mess up the gardens.'

Douglas stepped forward and spoke to the foxes. 'Is there any way that you could look in the dustbins without making a mess?'

The cub's dad laughed. 'We love making a mess.'

The fox cub laughed too. 'Scattering rubbish around the gardens is great fun.'

'It's not in our nature to be tidy,' said the cub's mum. 'But if it means that we can all live peacefully together then we will certainly try.'

The cub and his dad stopped laughing when they realized that Mum was being serious.

'We want to live in this neighbourhood,' she said. 'And so it's only fair that we show some respect to those that already live here.'

The cub and his dad said nothing. They knew that Mum was right.

Douglas turned to the cats. 'And why don't we say that scraps of food left out by humans are for everybody? The first animal who finds them can eat them.'

Nobody spoke, so Douglas decided to put his suggestions to a vote. 'All those in favour of these ideas, raise a paw in the air.'

The cats stared at the foxes and the foxes stared at the cats. After a few moments' silence, Fang raised a paw. Then Tiger did the same.

One by one paws were raised in approval.

'We have an agreement,' announced Clive triumphantly. 'I hereby announce details of my cat-fox agreement as drawn up by those cats and foxes present and witnessed by Fang the dog on this day the… what's today's date?'

'Get on with it,' said Bertie without opening his eyes.

'Rule one: Foxes may raid dustbins, but must do so tidily. Rule two: Scraps of food put out by humans may be taken by any animal, first come, first served. Any animal that breaks the cat-fox agreement shall be… shall be…'

'Shall be forced to come to another of these meetings,' said Bertie. 'And will have to listen to you talking all night.' Bertie stood up. 'You get more like a human every day.'

The other animals laughed and began to leave.

'I haven't finished yet,' said Clive. 'I have to make the closing speech.'

'I'll do that,' said Bertie. 'It's only one word. Goodnight!'

8

A Close Shave

For the next few days the cats checked all the
nearby gardens and were pleased to see that
none of them was messy. A couple of dustbins
had been pushed over, but none of the rubbish
had been thrown around. It seemed as if the
cat-fox agreement might just be a success.

One day Tiger and Douglas were on their
way to Clive's house, taking a short cut through
Mr Wright's garden, when Tiger spotted
something in the middle of the lawn. He ran
across the grass to have a closer look.

'Yum, yum,' he shouted. 'It's a sausage!'

'It's not like Mr Wright to leave food out for
us,' said Douglas.

'Perhaps he's happy because his garden
doesn't get messed up any more.'

Tiger was about to tuck in when the fox cub's dad leaped out of the bushes and pounced on top of him. He picked Tiger up in his mouth and flung him across the lawn.

'Leave that food alone!' spat the fox.

Douglas was furious.

'The rules! The rules!' he protested. 'Rule two of the cat-fox agreement clearly states that any animal can help themselves to food left out by humans.'

'Never mind the rules,' snapped the fox. 'Follow me.'

'But…'

'Quickly!'

The fox spoke so fiercely that Tiger and Douglas did exactly as they were told.

They followed the fox through the hedge into the next garden, where the fox cub's mum was waiting. It was the first time that Tiger and Douglas had seen the foxes in the daylight, and it was only now that they realized how beautiful they were.

Their coats were a rich reddish brown with flashes of white down their bellies and the lower half of their snouts. Their eyes, which had glowed green in the dark, were a beautiful orangey-yellow colour by day.

Douglas and Tiger spotted the fox cub lying on the ground. At first they thought he was sunbathing, but as they got closer they realized that something was wrong.

His eyes were closed, his tongue was hanging from the side of his mouth and he was gasping for air.

'What's the matter with him?' asked Tiger quietly.

'He's very ill,' said the cub's mum. 'He's been poisoned.'

'Poisoned?'

The cub's dad explained.

'One of the humans wants to drive all foxes out of the neighbourhood and has left poisoned food for us to eat.' He looked at Tiger. 'If you'd eaten that sausage you would have been poisoned too. And because you're so small the poison would have killed you.'

The fox had just saved Tiger's life!

'What are you going to do?' asked Douglas. 'How can you make him better?'

'We can't,' said the cub's dad. 'We have to move on. It's not safe for us to stay in this neighbourhood. He's too weak to travel with us and we'll have to leave him here.'

The cub's mum began to cry.

'But… but we can't leave him,' she sobbed. 'He'll die of hunger.'

The cub's dad was already heading out of the garden.

'Hurry, it is for the best.'

'No!' shouted Tiger. 'There must be

something we can do to save him.'

'He needs food and water to help build up his strength,' said Douglas. 'But any food that we find in the gardens may be poisoned.'

Tiger approached the fox cub and spoke gently. 'Can you hear me?'

Without opening his eyes, the cub nodded his head ever so slightly.

Tiger continued. 'If you can just stand up and follow me, I think I can help you. Can you do that?'

The cub summoned all his strength and managed to clamber to his feet. He began to sway from side to side and his mum had to support him to stop him from falling over.

'Well done,' said Tiger. 'Now follow me.'

'What are you doing?' asked the cub's dad. 'Where are you going?'

'I've got an idea,' said Tiger. 'Come on everybody, this way!'

9
⠶
Love Your Neighbour

The fox cub staggered forward with his mum by
his side and followed Tiger through the hedge.
Douglas was next, followed by the cub's dad.
Tiger led them through the neighbouring
gardens, collecting the other cats on the way.
Camilla was grooming herself on her patio.

'What's going on?' she asked.

'I'm not sure,' said Douglas. 'But Tiger seems
to know what he's doing.'

Camilla allowed her curiosity to get the better
of her. She got to her feet and pranced silently
through the gardens behind the other animals.
Her bell didn't ring. It had taken her only
a week to be able to move without making
a sound.

Clive was sitting on the step at the back of his

house and Bertie was dozing under his apple tree. They too joined the animal parade as it passed by.

After a few minutes, the cats and foxes arrived in Fang's back yard. The big dog had never had visitors before, and he was surprised and delighted to see all his new friends.

'Fang, we need your help,' said Tiger urgently. 'The fox cub has been poisoned. He's very ill and you are the only one who can save him.'

'Me?'

'He needs food and water. It's not safe for him to eat scraps from the gardens and we cats can't help because all our food is indoors. It would take too long for us to carry it outside.'

'What do you want me to do?' asked Fang.

'You're the only one who has his meals outside. I was wondering if you would be kind enough to share your dinner with him.'

Fang didn't need time to think about it.

'Always happy to help the neighbours,' he said, with a smile.

The animals hid behind the garage until

Fang's owner came out into the yard and placed bowls of food and water on the ground. When she had gone back inside the house, Tiger led the fox cub over to the food.

He watched as the cub tucked into the warm minced meat and gravy and washed it down with a drink of water.

'Now he needs rest,' said Tiger. 'He needs to sleep somewhere dry and safe.'

'What about my garage?' said Fang. 'Nobody ever goes in there.'

The garage door was slightly open and the animals went inside. The cub's dad stood on his hind legs and tugged a pair of overalls from a shelf. They dropped onto the floor and the cub's mum did her best to arrange them into a bed. The cub collapsed gratefully and closed his eyes immediately.

Fang spoke to the two big foxes. 'Perhaps you would like to spend the night here too,' he said. 'You will be safe here.'

'Thank you,' said the cub's dad.

'I'd like to stay too,' said Tiger. 'I want to look after the fox cub.'

'You have done enough already,' said the cub's mum. 'There's no need for you to stay.'

'But I want to,' insisted Tiger. 'Can I stay with him? Please?'

The cub's mum could see that it meant a lot to Tiger.

'Of course you can,' she said.

'Will you be all right, Tiger?' asked Douglas.

'I'll be all right. I just hope he gets better.'

'I'm sure he will,' said Clive. 'We'll see you in the morning.'

Fang followed Clive, Douglas, Bertie and Camilla out of the garage. The two foxes lay down on the floor as Tiger settled down next to the cub. The young fox was shaking slightly and

looked very feeble. It was hard to believe that he had been the bully known as 'the beast of the night'.

The cub opened his eyes and spoke quietly.

'I'm sorry, Tiger,' he said wearily. 'I'm sorry... I bullied you.'

Tiger didn't say anything.

'Why... why are you helping me? I was... horrible to you. Why are you helping me?'

'Your dad saved my life,' said Tiger. 'He showed me that you can care for others even if you don't know them very well. Even if they come from far away and you don't really understand the way they live, you can still care for them.'

Tiger pushed the edge of the overalls over the fox cub to keep him warm.

'Now try to rest,' whispered Tiger, but the cub was already fast asleep.

10

Another Courageous Cat

When the cub woke up in the morning, Tiger and the two big foxes were still watching over him. Fang was sitting outside the garage door. He'd been there all night, keeping guard. The other cats arrived early and waited in the garage until Fang's owner brought out his breakfast. It was a bowl of warm porridge and the cub gulped it down greedily. At lunchtime Fang donated his biscuits in warm milk. The young fox was getting stronger by the minute, and by the early evening he was able to walk from the garage without any help. Later, watched by his mum and dad and the cats, he and Fang shared a bowl of chicken soup.

'It's time for us to go now,' said the cub's dad. 'We must move on to another part of town.'

The cub suddenly looked very sad. 'Can't we stay a bit longer?'

'No, no,' said his mum. 'Poor Fang can't share his meals with you for ever.'

'That's right,' said his dad. 'I think you should say a big thank you to him.'

The fox cub thanked the big dog as he was told and then turned to Tiger.

'And thank you too, Tiger. I hope to see you again some time.'

'Goodbye,' said Tiger. 'Perhaps one day you can all come back and visit.'

'Perhaps one day we will,' said the cub's dad. 'Goodbye everybody and thank you.'

The cats had hardly finished saying goodbye before the foxes had quickly and quietly slipped round the back of the garage and were gone.

'Well done, Tiger,' said Clive. 'You're a hero.'

'I'm not the hero,' said Tiger. 'Fang is the hero. He shared his food with the fox cub and he came to the rescue of us cats when we were in trouble. And he did all that after I'd tried to blame everything on him. Thanks, Fang.'

Fang wagged his tail furiously.

'I think we should let Fang join our club,' said Douglas.

'But he's a dog,' said Camilla, pointing out the obvious.

'He would need special membership to join

the Courageous Cats' Club,' said Clive. 'And that would require a special meeting.'

'Yes, let's have a meeting!' shouted Bertie.

Clive was surprised and delighted at this show of enthusiasm and started his opening speech. Meanwhile Bertie and the other cats curled up, closed their eyes and began to catch up on all the sleep they had lost over the previous few nights. As Clive rambled on about club rules, Fang too struggled to keep his eyes open. When Clive decided to go over everything that had been talked about at earlier meetings Fang slumped to the floor with a thud. This didn't stop Clive from talking and, after about an hour, Fang officially became the first dog to become a member of the Courageous Cats' Club. He would have been very proud, if he hadn't been fast asleep!